GW00863812

MRS TIBBS

by

JOHN EVE

Illustrated by

ODELLO MARSHALL

TABB HOUSE

First published 1991
Tabb House, 11 Church Street, Padstow, Cornwall, PL28 8BG

ISBN 0 907018 78 5

FOR ADAM AND ROSIE

Typeset by St. George Typesetting, Redruth, Cornwall
Printed by
Quill Graphics, Padstow, Cornwall.

PREFACE

DEEP in the heart of South Devon, not very far from the blue Atlantic, lies a little secret valley at the foot of a plump Devon hillside. Mousehill is the name on the map although the village people call it Mouzle. Just beneath the faded name plate on an old farm gate is another notice. This proclaims to anyone lucky enough to find it that here you can have BED & BREAK. The FAST end of the board fell off long ago and was used to mend a hole at the bottom of the big barn door.

Here live Mr and Mrs Jackson with all their animals. There is a fine herd of red Devon cattle, a flock of sheep, all sorts of chickens, ducks and geese and a mischievous collie puppy who just will not grow up.

Below the grey stone farmhouse is a steep-sided lane that tries its hardest to get to the village but takes a very long time to get there. Here in the winter you can find violets and snowdrops flowering in the high banks. Somewhere, nearby, the infant river Avon hurries and chuckles through the oak trees and hazel thickets, impatient to get down to the sea. In the deeper pools, merging with the coloured pebbles, lie fat speckled trout and if you are very lucky Mrs Jackson will cook one for your breakfast.

Mr Jackson is rather old-fashioned – he doesn't care much for all those 'nasty chemicals' and sprays that are used on so many farms these days – which is why there are many butterflies dancing along the lane on warm spring days.

MOST of these stories are about one of the fattest sheep in Mr Jackson's flock and, of course, George, who manages to get his nose into almost everything. So take my hand, come with me to Mousehill Farm and let us meet Mrs Tibbs.

THE HOLE IN THE HEDGE

TWO large salty tears rolled down either side of Mrs Tibbs' woolly cheeks, racing each other to see which would be the first to jump off her chin. As they plopped onto the dead leaves below, they narrowly missed a tiny woodmouse who happened to be running along the bottom of the hedge. The mouse looked up anxiously at the dark grey cloud that seemed to hover above and stopped for a moment to dry her whiskers with a minute pair of paws The cloud rumbled ominously and the mouse had to jump sideways to avoid another large drop that splashed beside her. She might have gone on thinking that there was a storm overhead and rushed away to her neat little nest woven from dry grass and sheepswool, if the cloud hadn't given a loud despairing bleat. The mouse wrinkled her sensitive nose, this way and that, and was reassured by the comforting warm, woolly smell of Mrs Tibbs.

Mrs Tibbs had found a hole when she had been wandering along the hedgerow earlier in the morning, on the lookout for tasty herbs and bramble buds. She hadn't been able to resist pushing through the gap in the old thorn hedge to try to reach some tender young grass she could see on the other side. Now she was caught fast in a web of thorns and brambles that had become entangled in her thick fleece. The more she pushed the more she became entangled, while the few ivy leaves that she managed to reach were hardly enough to satisfy a person with such a large appetite.

The woodmouse climbed up a slender hazel stem to get a better view and had to hang on desperately with her tail and all four paws while an impatient Mrs Tibbs pushed harder and harder. The mouse's shrill squeaky voice tickled Mrs Tibbs' ear unbearably and she began to bleat loudly.

Bad news always travels quickly and before long several of Mrs Tibbs' friends gathered, some to offer advice, some to enjoy the sight of the fat and helpless Tibbs stuck fast, and some in the hope that there might be something to be gained from the situation. Amidst the general babble, bleating and woolly-headed confusion, with no one quite knowing what to do next, George the sheep-dog puppy arrived. Nobody liked George very much – he was always rushing at people and barking at them to make them hurry up. Even worse, at times he got so impatient that he was known to nip people on their bottoms! Mr Jackson, the farmer, was cross when this happened and would threaten to lock George up without any supper as a punishment.

All the sheep turned to face the naughty puppy and backed nervously up against the thorn hedge. Poor Mrs Tibbs was pushed further into the brambles. Nobody was listening to her complaining now – they were watching George with horror as he rushed up and down in excitement, barking loudly in their faces.

Suddenly there was a great cracking sound as three of Mr Jackson's stout fence posts on the other side of the hedge snapped under the strain.

"BAAAA!" shouted Mrs Tibbs, as she was pushed right through the hedge and the fence as well. She fell out onto a steep grassy bank. There was more crashing and breaking of branches as all the other sheep came tumbling through the hole, which was getting larger all the time. The last two sheep were able to walk right out of the field as George stood in the gap barking and jumping up and down.

There was a general helter-skelter and a grey tumbling of woolly balls as the runaway sheep rolled faster and faster down the hill. Mrs Tibbs,

being larger and fatter than anyone else, rolled the fastest of all. She wondered when it was all going to stop – one moment the sky had turned as green as grass, the next moment the field seemed to be all blue. She couldn't think where she was going as she bounced right over the gate at the bottom of the hill and into the lane.

Those sheep might have gone on bouncing and rolling down the lane and into the village if Farmer Jackson hadn't been bringing his cows home for milking at that very moment. By completely blocking the road the good-natured cows managed to avert what might have been a very nasty accident. The runaway sheep came to a sudden stop amid a lot of jostling, pushing and bleating and mooing, as everybody tried to explain at once.

Mrs Jackson was so amazed to see such a lot of animals coming into the farm-yard at milking time that she forgot to put any sugar in Mr Jackson's mug of tea. But Mrs Tibbs had a tasty-looking bunch of daffodils that she had plucked from the Vicar's garden as they passed, and all the other sheep were also busy chewing. Everybody seemed happy.

And George? Well, Mr Jackson found him fast asleep on the hay in the big barn – at least, I think he was fast asleep!

MRS TIBBS IS UNWELL

NO matter how hard Mr Jackson pushed at the barn door, it refused to open. George had managed to get the end of his nose through the gap underneath and was barking and huffing excitedly but that was no use either. The cows stood nearby, mooing impatiently and licking their noses because it was time for their breakfast.

"Bother and drat," said Mr Jackson, for he was late again that morning.

"I'll go and get help," he muttered and stamped off across the yard and into the farm kitchen.

Mrs Jackson had been doing the washing. She dried her hands on an extremely large apron and came out into the yard with Mr Jackson.

Together they put their shoulders to the big door and pushed and pushed and PUSHED. It was no good; the old door just would not move an inch.

"I shall have to get my ladder and get in through the loft at the back," said Mr Jackson, and he disappeared round the corner.

Mrs Jackson was thinking that perhaps she ought to go and make him a nice cup of tea when she suddenly heard the most extraordinary noises on the other side of the door. There was a grunting and a scrabbling, the sound of Mr Jackson's heavy breathing and one or two bothers and drats as well. Just as Mrs Jackson was about to call out, the big door swung open very slowly. Mr Jackson was sitting on a bale of hay, exhausted, glaring at the large woolly heap that he had managed to drag away from the door to the middle of the floor.

"BAAA," said the heap in a painful sort of way.

"Oh my dear life," said Mrs Jackson, throwing up her hands, "it's Mrs Tibbs!"

It was indeed Mrs Tibbs, larger than ever, and quite unable to move. Nearby were some upturned buckets and an empty sack that had once been filled with food for the cows' breakfasts.

"Drat me if her hasn't eaten the lot," complained Mr Jackson.

The cows said nothing at all but stared with their sad brown eyes.

George rushed up to bark but the woolly heap said nothing either. It had closed its eyes and looked dreadfully ill.

"Send for the veterinary," said Mrs Jackson, taking command, and Mr Jackson hurried off to the telephone.

"WE are not at all well, are WE?" said Mr Brown the vet, after he had examined Mrs Tibbs. He poked her on one side and then walked round her and prodded her on the other side.

"The other sheep are all right," assured Mr Jackson. "It's just this one."

"That's what I mean," replied Mr Brown as he opened a big black bag and got out an injection to give Mrs Tibbs. Mrs Tibbs kept her eyes shut tight and waited, but felt nothing at all.

"The poor lamb," said Mrs Jackson, sympathetically.

Then Mr Brown began to give instructions. Mrs Tibbs, her eyes still closed, heard words like "bicarbonate of soda," "Epsom salts" and "liquid paraffin" and "castor oil" and "TWICE a day," but she really didn't care or understand. She lay there in a great big soft woolly heap and sobbed quietly to herself.

For three days Mrs Jackson trotted out to the big barn with spoonfuls of medicine and bottles. On the fourth morning when she opened the door of the barn the large woolly heap had gone. There were a few whisps of hay from the bale that Mr Jackson had sat upon and two pieces of string – that was all. Mrs Jackson burst into tears.

"There, there, Midear," said Mr Jackson as he tried to comfort her. (He always called Mrs Jackson Midear when he was particularly pleased.) "George and I have just put Mrs Tibbs back in the field where she belongs. She must be much better 'cos she's eaten nearly all the cows' hay!"

Mrs Jackson went out to the field to look and there was Mrs Tibbs, quite her usual self, boasting about vets and injections and bicarbonate of soda to an admiring sheepy audience.

But I don't think she will be in such a hurry to help herself to all the cows' breakfast again, do you?

When Mr and Mrs Jackson sat down in Mrs Jackson's warm kitchen, they didn't think so either. And nowadays, just in case, the big barn door is always tied up carefully with a piece of string; even George, who can get into most things, is unable to get through.

MRS TIBBS TAKES A BATH

MR Jackson took a large gulp from his mug of tea, glared at the letter that had arrived in the post that morning and stamped out of the kitchen without finishing his egg and bacon.

Mrs Jackson ran after him with his packed lunch. "Don't forget your sandwiches," she said as she pushed a large packet into his hand.

"No time for market today, or even next week," grumbled Mr Jackson gloomily. "This letter from the Ministry," he went on, waving a large official brown envelope in front of a worried Mrs Jackson, "says we must dip every single sheep on the farm by the end of next week, according to the new regulations. Bother and drat – now I shall have to dig a great big hole in the orchard to make a new sheep dip," he complained.

"Won't the old one that we have always used, do?" suggested Mrs Jackson, trying to be helpful.

"No – it leaks and it isn't big enough now we have more sheep. I shall have to start work right away."

Mr Jackson pulled on his stoutest pair of boots and went to the barn to get a pick-axe and a large shovel. George the collie pup watched with great interest, and followed his master to the orchard. Mr Jackson, stripped of his jacket and pullover, dug deeper and deeper into the soft red soil and very soon a large mound of earth appeared under an old apple tree in the corner. George thought they might be digging for rabbits and was anxious to help. He began to dig in the large heap and earth cascaded from between his back legs as he scrabbled with his front paws. Most of it showered back into the hole on top of Mr Jackson.

"Bother and drat – go away, George!" he shouted, so crossly that George thought that perhaps it would be better if he went back to the yard to hunt for rats.

It took Mr Jackson three days to make the hole big enough for his purpose. Then he went to work with bricks and cement to line it and make it waterproof. Mrs Jackson came out from time to time with jugs of hot tea and cake and sandwiches and to make helpful suggestions. By the end of the week it was finished and a large, very impressive sheep dip was waiting in the corner of the orchard. All that remained was to put a fence around it and make a pen for the sheep.

On the last day Mr Jackson stood back to admire his handiwork. He had worked very hard to finish it in time and had forgotten to eat his sandwiches for lunch.

"That'll do nicely," he said to himself and stumped off wearily to the kitchen. It was peaceful and quiet in the old orchard now there were no more bothers and drats coming from the big hole under the apple tree.

The next morning life had returned to normal and Mr Jackson was cheerful as he finished his seventh slice of toast and marmalade at breakfast time. Mrs Jackson had gone out to feed the chickens and see to the sheep so he put three spoonfuls of sugar in his tea and picked up the paper. Suddenly there was a shrieking and wailing from outside, and Mrs Jackson rushed back across the farm-yard and into the kitchen without stopping to take off her wellington boots.

"Quickly, oh do come quickly!" she gasped as Mr Jackson put down his newspaper with a knowing "Bother and drat".

"Mrs Tibbs has completely disappeared!" sobbed Mrs Jackson.

(She was her favourite sheep although Mr Jackson often said that Tibbs was a dratted nuisance – behind Mrs Jackson's back, of course).

"All right," he said kindly. "She can't be far away," and they both went out to the orchard to look.

There was no sign of Mrs Tibbs, the gate was shut properly, there were no holes in the hedge and all the other sheep were there, grazing peacefully. But George was in the corner, barking furiously under the old apple tree. Mr and Mrs Jackson looked at each other.

"Of course," they exclaimed together, and rushed to the new sheep dip and peered over the edge. At the very bottom, wedged tightly between the sides was Mrs Tibbs. She seemed quite unconcerned as she chewed happily on Mr Jackson's forgotten sandwiches.

Mr Jackson fetched his tractor and tow-rope from the barn and they tied the end of the rope around Mrs Tibbs' neck and tried to pull her out. It was no use – she was quite impossibly stuck! Mrs Tibbs finished the last sandwich, looked hopefully into the empty paper bag and began to bleat. By this time the other sheep had gathered round the dip and were all baa-ing their encouragement. George hadn't stopped barking for a moment and even Mr Jackson's bother and drats could not be heard in the uproar.

It was Mrs Jackson's brilliant idea that saved the day. She unreeled the big hosepipe across the orchard and turned on the tap in the big barn so that the dip began to fill with water. It took quite a long time but

eventually Mrs Tibbs and the empty paper bag floated to the top of the bath and Mrs Tibbs was able to scramble out to safety. She shook herself vigorously, soaking Mr and Mrs Jackson and the other sheep, before she trotted off happily to continue grazing in the sunshine.

"Ah well," said Mrs Jackson, "at least we know the dip doesn't leak."

"Let's go and have a cup of tea," answered Mr Jackson.

GEORGE AND THE DRAGON

ALL through the long summer afternoon George had been uneasy. He had been listening to a strange roaring noise that seemed to be coming from the far end of the farm. He tried barking to attract Mrs Jackson's attention; she usually let him out if he went on long enough! No one came and the sinister noise continued. George decided he just had to investigate so he tried to dig a hole underneath the big barn door. It was no use; the floor was hard concrete and made his paws sore. Then he went to work on the door itself and began to bite and chew at a corner where his nose could poke out. He had sharp teeth and had soon made a pile of splinters and short strips of wood that he had torn from the bottom of the door. Then he could get most of his head out as well as his nose. Encouraged by this success, he worked even harder. The roaring was now getting louder and louder and eventually, almost overcome by impatience, he tried to squeeze through a gap that was barely large enough for Mrs Jackson's large tom cat, let alone a nearly full-grown sheep-dog. George was stuck. He scrabbled and squeezed. He clawed with his front paws and pushed with his back ones. Just when he thought he would have to stay there until Mr Jackson found him at supper time, there was a snap as his collar broke on a nail and he found himself free.

He ran along the farm-yard wall by the garden where no one would see him. Then he jumped over the gate at the end of the yard and was away. The noise was still there, sometimes louder and sometimes fainter, a sort of clanking, roaring and humming all rolled into one. George had never heard such a strange animal and as he got closer he thought he had better be careful in case it was dangerous. He crept on his tummy all the way through the orchard. Mrs Tibbs saw him and snorted and stamped her foot to warn the other sheep. They came skippetty-hop across the grass but George didn't notice them – he was intent on more serious business.

He slipped under the gate at the far end of the orchard and into the field where Mr Jackson's cows were grazing. They lifted their heads and mooed after him but George did not hear them. The noise was getting much louder now and George trembled with excitement as he

peeped cautiously through the hedge and into the field of corn beyond. There, rumbling ominously through the gateway was an enormous red DRAGON. George could not wait a moment longer; he scrambled through the hedge, bravely rushed up to the monster and barked and barked and BARKED. But the huge animal was not going to be chased off. It seemed to hesitate for a moment and then, puffing out a cloud of black smoke, lumbered into Mr Jackson's barley field. George took his stand firmly in the corn just inside the gate, and refused to move. He stood his ground, growling very fiercely indeed. The red dragon stopped as if it was confused, and the whirring, clanking and humming noise died away. A man in overalls who was riding on top of it called out to George to get out of the way, but he dared not come down. George went on barking, encouraged now that he seemed to have the upper hand.

It was at this moment that Mrs Jackson went to the yard to feed the hens and to collect the eggs. At once she noticed the hole under the big barn door. There were a few tufts of black and white fur, a broken collar caught on an old rusty nail but no sign of George himself. Mrs Jackson dropped her bucket and ran into the kitchen to tell Mr Jackson, who was having his cup of tea.

"Bother and drat; what is that George up to this time?" complained Mr Jackson. He always called him 'that George' when he was cross with him. Mrs Jackson explained about the hole under the barn door and the broken collar. They got into the Land-Rover.

"We had better find him before he gets up to any more of his mischief," said Mr Jackson gloomily. He lifted a hand to his ear and listened for a moment.

"The combine next door seems to have broken down again." They looked at each other. They had both heard, in place of the combine's noise, the unmistakeable sound of George, barking in the distance.

"Oh dear; it sounds as if it's coming from the top field. What is he doing so far from home?" wailed Mrs Jackson.

Mr Jackson drove up the lane as fast as he could. They arrived at the field at the top to find George, bravely barring the way to a large red combine-harvester that had tried to get into Mr Jackson's cornfield.

"Hey, what are you doing in my cornfield?" shouted Mr Jackson to the driver, who seemed to be too frightened to get down from the machine. Mrs Jackson put George into the back of the Land-Rover, where he continued growling. Ernie Hoskin, the driver, tried to explain, but as he did so he realised that he had made a dreadful mistake: he had driven into the wrong field of corn. He was supposed to be harvesting on the farm next door and had driven through Mr Jackson's gateway instead.

"Never mind," said Mr Jackson, kindly. "Come with us and we'll telephone our neighbours to find out which field you should be cutting next.''

While they all drove down to Mousehill Farm Ernie made friends with George.

''What a lucky thing George investigated,'' said Mrs Jackson.

As he stroked George's ears, Ernie agreed.

Mr Jackson said that he could easily mend the barn door and George got another bowl of nice warm milk for supper that evening, although he was not quite sure why.

SPOTTY MULDOON

IN the old days, before there were tractors and combine harvesters at Mousehill Farm, Mr Jackson's father and his grandfather had great shire horses to do the farm work. They were kept in the stables alongside the big barn. It was a sad day when they went, to make way for a new tractor, but then Mr Jackson had made the old building into a very comfortable place to keep pigs. This is where Spotty Muldoon lived with his friends. You may think that this is an odd sort of name for a pig, but Muldoon was an odd sort of pig. He certainly was very spotty and also quite the naughtiest pig that had ever come to Mousehill Farm.

The pigs' house, as Mr and Mrs Jackson now called it, had a solid oak door. This had been lined with corrugated iron to stop the pigs (who have very strong teeth) from gnawing their way out. Muldoon had already tasted freedom – the first time was when he arrived on a lorry from market and had slipped away between Mr Jackson's legs. He had run round and round the yard, squealing with delight, followed by all his friends. Then he had found the gate into the farm garden, and I leave you to imagine the dreadful damage those naughty pigs did before Mr Jackson got a broom and Mrs Jackson a clothes prop, with which they managed to drive them to the pigs' house and shut them in.

Mrs Tibbs and the other sheep had no great opinion of the pigs. The second time that Muldoon led them on the rampage was when Mr Jackson had gone to clean out their house. They pushed him rudely out of the way as he went in with an armful of clean straw for their beds and scampered down to the orchard. They had a marvellous time chasing the poor sheep round and round the apple trees until Muldoon discovered the rotting windfall apples. He had eaten so many of these that he became quite ill and had to be taken back to the pigs' house in a wheel-barrow. 'And serve him right,' thought Mrs Tibbs, who was out of breath with so much excitement and running around.

But Spotty Muldoon had not met George – that is, not until the third escape with his friends, when he lifted the old door right off its hinges with his nose. Sixteen excited pigs, led of course by Muldoon, squeezed under the farm gate and ran away down the lane.

Mrs Tibbs saw them tear past the orchard and she stamped her foot and snorted a warning. The sheep all gathered in a nervous bleating group in the corner by the new dip. There was a great quacking from the ducks, who had sought the safety of the farm pond. The hens were shrieking and cackling in fright on the roof of the cow shed and refusing to come down again. The cows were mooing although it was nowhere near milking time, while George was barking furiously and scratching at the big barn door. When Mr and Mrs Jackson returned home from market a little while later, the whole farm was in uproar.

Mrs Jackson said that she was sure a fox had been after the poultry so Mr Jackson let George out of the barn and went to get his gun. George didn't wait, and with his nose to the ground disappeared on the trail of the naughty runaways.

The pigs had gone all the way down the lane, crossed the bridge over the river and had just arrived at the Vicarage, when George caught up with them.

Muldoon stood in the neat drive and admired the scarlet geraniums that lined the path on one side and the rows of succulent vegetables in the kitchen garden on the other. He hesitated for a moment, wondering which ones they should sample first.

George had jumped right over the hedge into the garden, startling the Vicar's wife who was busy weeding, skirted the well-kept lawn and come face to face with Muldoon and his gang. Muldoon's shifty little eyes watched as George crept slowly forward on his tummy. He ignored the warning signs as George's ears flattened and his lip curled up a little to expose sharp white teeth. Muldoon gave one of his fiercest grunts – no one was going to frighten him – and he took another step forward. That was when George bit him, right on the end of his nose. Muldoon squealed and turned tail as George bit him again on his fat bottom. The pigs scampered out of the garden, back over the bridge and all the way along the lane to the farm. George brought up the rear, making sure that no one lagged behind.

Mrs Jackson was just opening the farm gate to let Mr Jackson out in his Land-Rover to look for the runaways when the gang of pigs hurtled past them and ran straight into the pigs' house. George mounted guard until Mr Jackson had put the door back on its hinges and fastened it securely.

"Well I never . . ." exclaimed Mrs Jackson. "I never thought that George would turn out to be a Pig Dog as well!"

"Very useful," agreed Mr Jackson. "But that dratted Muldoon will have to go."

The very next morning Spotty Muldoon was loaded into the back of

the Land-Rover and taken to market. Mr Jackson was so pleased with George that he let him ride on the front seat (although this was partly in case Muldoon caused any more trouble on the way).

George was excited – he had been to market only once before in his life but he remembered the bustle and exciting sounds and smells.

When they got to the market Mr Jackson put the pig in a pen all by himself. He looked sad and lonely and it was a subdued Muldoon that eventually came up for sale.

"Who will give me a bid for this spotted pig?" sang out the auctioneer.

There was silence. The auctioneer tried again, but no one seemed to want Muldoon.

When Mr Jackson came back later Muldoon was still in his pen, unsold and alone. They had to load him in the Land-Rover again and take him back to the farm. As the door of the pigs' house was bolted securely behind him Muldoon seemed pleased and grateful to be back with his friends.

"Never mind," said Mrs Jackson. "That pig has learned his lesson and won't be any trouble now." George and Mr Jackson looked at each other while Mr Jackson sipped his mug of tea in the kitchen. They weren't quite so sure!

THE RUSTLERS

EVER since Mrs Jackson had discovered early one morning that the gate to the orchard was wide open and that all the sheep, including Mrs Tibbs, had disappeared, the Jacksons had been distraught. Mr Jackson had been out all day in his Land-Rover, scouring the countryside and all the little lanes and by-ways but hadn't seen any sign of them. Mrs Jackson had taken George and looked in all the barns and in the sheep dip too, without success. Then she had been busy on the telephone asking the neighbours, but no one had seen or heard of any straying or lost sheep.

At last Mr Jackson took off his boots and sat down wearily in his armchair in front of the television. Mrs Jackson had gone to the kitchen to make him a nice pot of tea and to cook his supper, although he said he was far too worried about the sheep to eat anything.

''Bother and drat,'' he said sadly to himself as he switched on the evening news. A moment later he sat up with a start, for he found himself looking straight at the familiar face of Mrs Tibbs on the television screen.

''Perhaps I'm dreaming,'' he said to wake himself up – but there was no doubt at all. There, quite unmistakably, was a fat and contented Mrs Tibbs, chewing nonchalantly on a sandwich and being interviewed by a reporter. Mrs Jackson heard the commotion and rushed in from the kitchen, spilling the tea all over the carpet, as she heard Mrs Tibbs bleating at the cameras.

''Oh my dear life – the poor lamb!'' sobbed Mrs Jackson.

''And this very brave sheep,'' continued the announcer, ''by her gallant action today, helped the police to arrest a gang of sheep rustlers that has evaded capture for several months.''

He went on to explain how Mrs Tibbs had broken into the cab of a lorry that was transporting the stolen sheep, causing the driver to veer off the motorway and crash on the grass bank, and then sat on him until the police arrived.

''His accomplice was caught after a chase across nearby fields. There

has been a complete blockage of the motorway and a tailback of traffic for nearly ten miles,'' he concluded. A police helicopter had been called out to assist in the rounding up of the remaining sheep and the control of the traffic. Fortunately no one had been hurt in the incident.

It was all very heroic.

Mr and Mrs Jackson watched in amazement and relief at pictures of the rest of their sheep safely penned in a field by the motorway and the wreckage of the lorry being towed away. There were more shots of Mrs Tibbs accepting digestive biscuits from a grateful Chief Inspector.

THE real truth about the heroism was rather different. Mrs Tibbs and her companions had been lured from their field in the night by a cunningly laid trail of sheep 'nuts' that led right into the back of the thieves' lorry. Once they were inside and busily filling themselves up with hay and more food, the door had been slammed on them and they were driven away. It had seemed ages to Mrs Tibbs that they were being driven along and she began to feel hungry again.

Then she caught the unmistakable smell of sandwiches coming through a small crack in the front of the lorry.

She pushed and PUSHED to try to get a glimpse through the wooden partition and discover where the delicious smell was coming from, when the boarding gave way with a crack. Mrs Tibbs suddenly found herself in the cab with the thieves, jammed very tightly between the driver and the steering wheel. She tried to turn this way and that to get at the food but only succeeded in making the lorry veer from one side of the motorway to the other. There was a sound of angry motor horns, a few heavy bumps and finally a crash, as the lorry mounted the bank and fell over onto its side. Mrs Tibbs sat happily where she landed, ignoring the muffled shouts that were coming from somewhere beneath her thick woolly coat: she had found the sandwiches!

THE HARVEST FESTIVAL

MR and Mrs Jackson were in a terrible hurry. They had been busy since daybreak, running to and fro between the kitchen and Mr Jackson's Land-Rover, which was parked in the farmyard. It was being loaded with cabbages and potatoes from the garden, turnips that Mr Jackson had dug from the field the night before, a sack of corn from the barn and last of all, a basket of new laid eggs and a crisp brown loaf that Mrs Jackson had baked especially for the Harvest Festival.

''Bother,'' said Mr Jackson as he struggled to lace up his new brown boots – he hadn't even had time for his second cup of tea at breakfast time. Mrs Jackson was in the hall putting on her best hat and admiring herself in the mirror.

"Come along, Midear," said Mr Jackson. "We mustn't be late at the Church." He wanted to be there early to arrange his farm produce nicely.

They climbed into the old Land-Rover and drove down the lane towards the village. Mr Jackson was in such a hurry that he didn't notice that the gate to the meadow was wide open and swinging in the wind.

There seemed to be a great commotion going on at the church when they arrived – two choir boys nearly knocked Mrs Jackson over as they dashed out of the gate from the churchyard.

"Drat," said Mr Jackson, as the biggest turnip fell from his arms and rolled slowly down the path and onto the road. At the same time he was trying to balance the sack of corn on his back.

"Well, I never did!" exclaimed Mrs Jackson as she tried to put her hat straight again.

At that moment the Vicar rushed out of the church. "Help, HELP – send for the Bishop!" he cried. "It's a poltergeist!"

"A polty-what?" asked Mrs Jackson, quite alarmed.

"It's knocked down my pulpit and destroyed the flower arrangements," shouted the Vicar. (He was very excited.)

"And my lovely vegetables have all been chewed and nibbled," wailed the Vicar's wife as she tried to dry her tears on his surplice.

Mr Jackson put down his sack of corn, went into the porch and very slowly peered round the door into the church. What a dreadful sight met his eyes! There were vegetables scattered all over the aisle. A large vase of chrysanthemums had been broken and the vicar's lectern was leaning over at an alarming angle.

The large white poltergeist did not appear to notice Mr Jackson – it was too busy eating the last carrot from a basket of vegetables that had once been the pride of the vicarage garden.

"No need to send for the Bishop – I will deal with this," said a grim-faced Mr Jackson to the Vicar as he came out of the porch.

"Oh good man, good man," and "How brave," said the Vicar and his wife together.

"Do be careful," warned Mrs Jackson anxiously.

Mr Jackson got his big crook from the Land-Rover and went straight back into the church.

If anybody had looked round the corner of the church wall a few moments later, they would have seen a puffing and grunting Mr Jackson pulling a large woolly poltergeist out of the vestry door and with many bothers and drats, struggling to load it into the back of his Land-Rover.

After a short time, Mr Jackson reappeared and announced that it was now quite safe to go back into the church. The congregation, which had now arrived, applauded, and Mrs Jackson felt very proud as she followed her husband and the Vicar inside. They all set to work and order was soon restored. They put the chrysanthemums and the other flowers into the font. Mr Jackson and the Vicar managed to push the lectern back to its proper place and the Harvest Festival began only half an hour late.

After the service it seemed that Mr Jackson was in an even greater hurry to get home again. Without waiting to shake the Vicar's hand, he rushed Mrs Jackson to a rather hot and steamed-up Land-Rover.

"Whatever happened to the Polty-goose?" asked a mystified Mrs Jackson.

"It's quite safe in the back," said Mr Jackson, who was very relieved to be on his way home at last.

Mrs Jackson turned round rather apprehensively.

"BAA," said the poltergeist.

"Oh my dear life! It's Mrs Tibbs," she said.

THE GREAT SNOW

WHEN Mrs Jackson woke up that morning, she knew that something was different. There was a bright white light coming through the curtains but there were none of the familiar farm-yard sounds that usually awoke her early in the morning. There was no clucking of hens or mooing from the cow shed. Even George, who always found something to bark about, was silent. It seemed that a great hush had descended on the farm. Mr Jackson put on his slippers and pulled back the curtain.

"Bother and drat," he exclaimed. "It's bin snawing!"

They both hurried downstairs to the kitchen and opened the back door to the yard, before even putting the great black kettle on the stove for their cup of tea.

It had indeed been snowing – snowing hard all night and there was still quite a blizzard whirling the white flakes round the yard outside. Everything was under a thick white blanket, and an enormous drift was heaped up against the doorway and the farmhouse wall. Mr Jackson pulled on his great big wellington boots, took his stick from the corner and struggled to get his arms into his thick winter overcoat. Mrs Jackson tied her warmest scarf tightly over her head and round her ears and looked in the drawer of the dresser for her woolly mittens. They stepped out into a strangely quiet and muffled world and struggled across the yard. Mr Jackson opened the barn door and George rushed out in a state of great excitement. He had never seen snow before and promptly fell into the snowdrift and almost disappeared.

"We must get the sheep into the shelter of the barn," called Mr Jackson, as he moved a sack of corn out of the way and propped the door open.

Mrs Jackson had already gone to the gate of the orchard. "Sheep, sheep, SHEEP," she cried as loudly as she could, and then "Come on, come on". Nothing seemed to move in the confusing whiteness and there was not a sheep to be seen. Then, after a moment one of the snowdrifts seemed to shake and move and suddenly some of the sheep appeared, looking like walking Christmas cakes covered with a deep layer of frosty icing. Mr Jackson began to count as they pushed and jostled to get through the gateway to the farm-yard.

"Bother and drat!" said Mr Jackson as he counted to forty-nine and looked in vain for one more sheep to appear. "There's one missing," he called out to Mrs Jackson.

Mrs Jackson came into the yard and counted the flock as well: forty-eight the first time and forty-nine the second, because one of the sheep had already found the safety and warmth of the big barn.

"Oh dear – I can't see Mrs Tibbs!" cried a worried Mrs Jackson.

It was very difficult to see who was who, with such a covering of snow stuck to their woolly coats, but Mrs Jackson was right – Mrs Tibbs was indeed missing.

"Us'll have to search the orchard," grumbled Mr Jackson. "I expect she'll be sheltering along the garden wall or else under the old apple tree," he muttered.

"We'll take George – he's always good at finding things," said Mrs Jackson; "even if he isn't supposed to," she added.

George felt very pleased to be wanted, and dashed in and out of the gate like a mad thing, falling into another big snowdrift. It was almost impossible to get round the orchard, the snow was so deep, while the garden wall had completely disappeared under a great white bank. Mr and Mrs Jackson called here and called there and looked under the apple trees, but there was no sign of Mrs Tibbs. Everything looked the same under the cover of the snow.

George had disappeared, too. He was very busy digging one of his spectacular holes in the middle of the biggest snowdrift. A steady white stream flew from between his back legs as he dug deeper and deeper. The tip of his tail was showing for a moment as Mr Jackson arrived then, quite suddenly, that was gone as well. Mr Jackson called to his wife and together they peered into the depths of a large dark hole. They could just hear some excited but muffled yips and barks, when there was a loud thump and George was propelled backwards right out of the snowdrift. A moment later a strong smell of sheep was followed by Mrs Tibbs' angry face as she glared out at them all. Mr Jackson scraped more snow from round the side of the hole in case she was stuck but Mrs Tibbs just would not come out. Mrs Jackson had gone, but returned in a few moments with a bucket and some crushed oats. Mrs Tibbs allowed herself to be coaxed out for a moment, took two hurried mouthfuls and turned back into the hole. She gave a soft bleat and then to the Jacksons' surprise, out clambered a small fat lamb. Mrs Tibbs bleated again and a second lamb appeared, followed closely by a third.

"Oh my dear life! She's had triplets!" shouted a delighted Mrs Jackson. "The poor dear must be starved."

Mrs Tibbs agreed, and when Mr Jackson had managed to pick up all three lambs, putting one under each arm and the third down the front of his overcoat, the procession struggled back across the orchard to the big barn. George brought up the rear at a safe distance; he didn't want to be 'bunted' again. Mrs Tibbs was given a pen all to herself with her lambs and of course some more oats and lots of hay.

"What a good dog," said Mr Jackson kindly, as he gave George a large bowl of warm milk as a reward. George felt enormously proud to have been so useful.

Then Mr and Mrs Jackson went into the kitchen for their breakfast and a nice cup of hot tea.